KU-093-392

SHARE A STORY

Walking Through the Jungle

Introduction

One of the best ways you can help
your children learn and learn to read
is to share books with them. Here's why:

• They get to know the **sounds**, **rhythms** and **words**
used in the way we write. This is different from how we
talk, so hearing stories helps children learn how to read.

• They think about the **feelings** of the characters
in the book. This helps them as they go about
their own lives with other people.

• They think about the **ideas** in the book. This helps
them to understand the world.

• Sharing books and listening to what your children
say about them shows your children that you care
about them, you care about what they think
and who they are.

Michael Rosen

Michael Rosen
Writer and Poet
Children's Laureate (2007-9)

First published 1993 by Walker Books Ltd
87 Vauxhall Walk, London SE11 5HJ

This edition published 2011

2 4 6 8 10 9 7 5 3 1

© 1993 Julie Lacome
Concluding notes © CLPE 2011

The right of Julie Lacome to be identified as author/illustrator of this work
has been asserted by her in accordance with the Copyright, Designs and Patents Act 1988

This book has been typeset in Garamond

Printed in China

All rights reserved. No part of this book may be reproduced, transmitted
or stored in an information retrieval system in any form or by any means,
graphic, electronic or mechanical, including photocopying, taping and recording,
without prior written permission from the publisher.

British Library Cataloguing in Publication Data:
a catalogue record for this book is available from the British Library

ISBN 978-1-4063-3519-4

www.walker.co.uk

Walking Through the Jungle

Julie Lacome

WALKER BOOKS
AND SUBSIDIARIES
LONDON · BOSTON · SYDNEY · AUCKLAND

Walking through the jungle,
What do you see?
Can you hear a noise?
What could it be?

SSSsss

Over there!
A snake
looking
for his tea.

Leaping through the jungle,
What do you see?
Can you hear a noise?
What could it be?

Over there!
A lion
looking
for his tea.

Running through the jungle,
What do you see?
Can you hear a noise?
What could it be?

trump trump

Over there!
An elephant
looking
for his tea.

Swinging through the jungle,
What do you see?
Can you hear a noise?
What could it be?

chitter chatter

Over there!
A monkey
looking
for his tea.

Wading through the jungle,
What do you see?
Can you hear a noise?
What could it be?

snap snap

Over there!
A crocodile
looking
for his tea ...

Hope it isn't
me!

Sharing Stories

Sharing stories together is a pleasurable way to help children learn to read and enjoy books. Reading stories aloud and encouraging children to talk about the pictures and join in with parts of the story they know well are good ways to build their interest in books. They will want to share their favourite books again and again. This is an important part of becoming a successful reader.

Walking Through the Jungle takes children on an adventure where they are explorers meeting one wild animal after another. Here are some ways you can share this book:

• You can encourage them to use the clues about each animal to guess "Who can it be?" before they turn the page to find out.

• Together you can play "find the animal" games, searching through the book to find the animal that roars or the animal with tusks, two legs or no legs.

• Children can join in with the strong rhyme and tune, "singing" the parts of the story they remember.

• Children can use animal toys to retell the story, using their own words as well as phrases they know from the book.

• You can play your own "Who can it be?" game when you're out for a walk (or adventure), singing your way through the story and taking it in turns to give sound clues (*roarrr!*) to the next mystery animal you encounter. Children might add different animals and use other kinds of clues, such as acting out the way an animal moves or saying something about it.

SHARE A STORY
A First Reading Programme
From Pre-school to School

Beginnings – 2 years+

Look Out, Suzy Goose — Petr Horáček

Walking Through the Jungle — Julie Lacome

Hello, Goodbye — David Lloyd, Louise Voce

Penny Dale — TEN IN THE BED

THIS IS THE BEAR — Sarah Hayes, Helen Craig

The Big Wide-Mouthed Frog — Ana Martín Larrañaga

Early Steps – 3 years+

A New House for Mouse — Petr Horáček

The Train Ride — June Crebbin, Stephen Lambert

THE OTHER DAY I MET A BEAR — Russell Ayto

Old MacDonald Had a Farm

The Tiger and the Jackal — Vivian French, Alison Bartlett

Zed's Bread — Mick Manning, Brita Granström

Next Steps – 4 years+

The Hairy Toe — Daniel Postgate

The True Story of Humpty Dumpty — Sarah Hayes, Charlotte Voake

BEANS ON TOAST — Paul Dowling

Over in the Meadow — A Counting Rhyme — Louise Voce

Polly Dunbar — Dog Blue

Night-night, Knight And Other Poems — Michael Rosen, Sue Heap

Taking Off – 5 years+

"Have You Seen the Crocodile?" — Colin West

HANDA'S SURPRISE — Eileen Browne

The Ravenous Beast — Niamh Sharkey

One, Two, Flea! — Allan Ahlberg, Colin McNaughton

Dinosaurs' Day Out — Nick Sharratt

The Old Woman and the Red Pumpkin — Betsy Bang, Rachel Merriman

Sharing the best books makes the best readers

WALKER BOOKS

www.walker.co.uk